Zoë
and the
Mermaids

D0308501

43

Zoë
and the
Mermaids

First published in Great Britain in 2006
by Piccadilly Press Ltd.,
5 Castle Road, London NW1 8PR
www.piccadillypress.co.uk

Text and illustration copyright © Jane Andrews, 2006

All rights reserved. No part of this publication may be reproduced, stored in a retrieval
system, or transmitted, in any form or by any means, electronic, mechanical, photocopying or
otherwise, without prior permission of the copyright owner.

The right of Jane Andrews to be recognised as Author and Illustrator of this work
has been asserted by her in accordance with the Copyright, Designs and Patents Act 1988.

Text designed by Louise Millar
Colour reproduction by Dot Gradations Ltd UK
Printed in China

ISBN: 1 85340 833 6 (hardback)
1 85340 838 7 (paperback)

EAN: 9 781853 408335 (hardback)
9 781853 408380 (paperback)

1 3 5 7 9 10 8 6 4 2

A catalogue record of this book
is available from the British Library

**EAST SUSSEX
SCHOOLS LIBRARY SERVICE**

29-Jun-06	PETERS
569809	

Jane Andrews has two sons and lives in High Wycombe in Buckinghamshire.
She has written nine books for Piccadilly Press
including the eight Zoë titles and MILLY AT MAGIC SCHOOL.

Other Zoë titles available from Piccadilly Press:

ZOË AT FAIRY SCHOOL
ZOË THE TOOTH FAIRY
ZOË AND THE FAIRY CROWN
ZOË AND THE WITCHES' SPELL
ZOË AND THE DRAGON
ZOË AND THE MAGIC HARP
ZOË AND THE FAIRY MEDICINE

Zoë
and the
Mermaids

Jane Andrews

Piccadilly Press • London

At last it was the summer holidays, and the fairies were enjoying a day at the fairies' special beach, where the sun always shines, and the sea is just the right temperature for swimming in.

As soon as they arrived the fairies scattered along the beach, splashing, playing and swimming.

After Zoë and Pip went swimming in the sea, they decided to
build a sandcastle.
'Wouldn't it be great if we saw some mermaids here?' Zoë
said, as they made their way back to the Fairy Queen.
'We'll have to keep an eye out,' Pip replied.

They told the Fairy Queen that they were going further down the beach where there were fewer fairies and more sand, and that they were on the lookout for mermaids.

'I'm not certain you'll see any mermaids . . .' the Fairy Queen said, 'but see if you can find me a pretty shell instead.'

Zoë and Pip found the perfect spot and started digging.

The sandcastle got bigger and bigger. They were so busy that they didn't see the large crab looking at their spade.

Suddenly the crab grabbed the spade in one of his claws and raced towards the water's edge.

Zoë and Pip ran after him as fast as they could.

They lost sight of the crab as they reached
the water's edge.
'Let's look over the other side of this rock
and see if he is there,' suggested Zoë.
They very carefully flew and climbed up
the steep slope.

When they got to the top, they couldn't believe their eyes.
Right there in front of them was a real, live mermaid!

But then they heard the sound of crying, so they climbed
down the rocks to ask what was wrong.
'My sister is stuck under some coral and I can't get her out,'
sobbed the mermaid. 'The sea cucumber is staying with her
while I try to find help.'

Zoë and Pip knew right away that they had to help. They used their magic to make bubbles over their heads so they could breathe underwater, and used their wands to light their way.

Under the water it was beautiful. Zoë and Pip were enchanted by all the colourful sea creatures, but there was no time to linger. They had to get to the mermaid's sister.

When they reached the trapped mermaid, they tried together
with all their might to pull her out.

But it was no good, she was stuck fast. Just when Zoë was coming up with another idea, something very large floated over them.

'Quick, hide!' said Pip. 'It looks like a . . .'

'SHARK!'

The shark swam directly over them, casting a huge shadow and everything went dark. The fairies, the mermaid and the sea cucumber held their breath as the shark slowly moved past.

It was a long time after the shark had passed before anyone moved or made a sound.

'I think it is safe now,' said Zoë. 'Why don't we try some magic?'

The mermaid seemed to move a little and Zoë and Pip concentrated very hard. But just as they thought she was starting to come free . . .

. . . the shark returned!

'Quickly, one more go!' shouted Zoë, and they concentrated with all their might on the wands and the mermaid struggled free. Zoë and Pip turned to face the shark.

'Now wave your wand hard,' Pip said. 'I think if we can cast the right spell all the shark's teeth will fall out.'

Both fairies waved their wands for all they were worth, and
watched as the shark's teeth came loose and drifted to the
ocean floor.
The surprised shark swam away as fast as he could.
'Phew!' said Zoë. 'That was close.'

The mermaids were so happy to be safe that they gave Zoë and Pip as many hugs as they could. And the rescued mermaid gave the fairies her necklace of shells to share.

SWOOSH!

By now Zoë and Pip knew they needed to get back to the other fairies so they said goodbye to the sea cucumber, held on tightly to the mermaids' tails, and *SWOOSH* . . .

Moments later they were back on the beach.
They popped their bubbles, and waved goodbye
to the mermaids.
'Look, Pip!' exclaimed Zoë. 'There's our spade!'
The sea seemed to be returning it to them with
the waves.

Back at the beach, Zoë and Pip presented the Fairy Queen
with the shell necklace.
'How lovely!' the Fairy Queen said. 'Now isn't finding beautiful
shells better than finding mermaids?'
Zoë and Pip looked at each other and smiled.